the stor

Ma

WRITTEN AND ILLUSTRATED BY

TINNI CHATTERJEE

To Raghav and Aditya,
Thank you being my inspiration for this book
series. Hope you love reading this and learning
more about "Namo-Namo". May the curious
little boys in you find answers to your queries.

Happy Reading!

on earth had become very evil.
"Oh, Look at them!", roared
Brahma, the creator. "How corrupt
and wicked! I feel like destroying
all that I have created".

that!"

"Oh, I do!", said *Brahma* determined.

"But…but not all of them are corrupt!" reasoned *Vishnu*. "Look at Manu for example.."

They were talking about a wise and kind man named *Manu*. He was an honourable person who led his life with morals.

earth" repeated Brahma. "If *Manu* is a good man, I'll spare him. But the others have to go!"

"But....", started *Vishnu* but *Brahma* cut him short.

arguing with *Brahma*. The best he
can do is save *Manu*. and create a
new mankind through him.
So, he set up a test to prove *Manu's*
worth to *Brahma*.

form of a fish and. This was his *Matysa* avatar – the first time he came to earth.

up to *Manu*, while he washed in the river.

"*Manu*", *Matsya* called out. (Yes, those days fishes and humans could talk to each other)

"How can I help you?" asked *Manu*.

"You see, I am a tiny helpless baby fish. So many large fishes want to eat me! Can you please, find a way to keep me safe?", pleaded *Matsya*.

carefully picked up the fish in his palms and placed it gently in a puddle close to his home.

"Don't worry little fish." he said to *Matsya* "You are safe here."

Matsya looked at *Brahma,* who had been watching all this. He looked astonished.

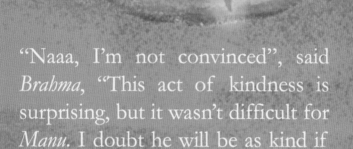

"Naaa, I'm not convinced", said *Brahma,* "This act of kindness is surprising, but it wasn't difficult for *Manu.* I doubt he will be as kind if he had to put in an effort."

watched as Manu tended to every
need of the fish.
Matsya began to grow.

In fact, *Matsya* grew so much that
the puddle became small for it.
So, *Manu* built a pond for the fish
and moved it there.

But *Matsya* kept growing. Soon *Manu* had to move him back into the river.
But *Manu* didn't stop caring for it.

Brahma was immensely pleased but *Vishnu* had one last test.

Next day *Matsya* swam up to *Manu* and said "*Manu,* Can you take me to the ocean. I want to live in the comfort of the warm ocean."

Manu "It will not be easy to take
a big fish like you all the way
there"

"I know. And that is why I trust
only you", replied *Matsya*.

It will be a long and exhausting journey.

But he looked at *Matsya's* face and his heart melted.
"Ok, I'll take you there", he said.

water, placed *Matsya* gently into it and started walking towards the ocean. *Manu* needed all his strength to carry *Matsya* to the ocean.

being so selfless and caring!

Vishnu smiled at *Brahma*. He turned to *Manu* and said, "My dear *Manu*. You are a great man. The time has come to tell you the truth. I am no fish. I am *Vishnu*. I have been testing you and you have passed with flying colors".

Manu was stunned.

"Wh…wh...what!", was all he managed to say.

—

"A terrible flood is going to come to cleanse the earth. Everything will be destroyed."

Manu finally found his voice. "Why are you telling me this?", he asked.

"Because, you are the chosen one!" replied *Vishnu*.

"You must build a mighty ark. When the rains start, board the ark and take a pair each, of all the living creatures and seeds of all plants. Take the seven *gurus* (*Saptarishi*). And stay put till I tell you to come out."

Manu bowed to *Vishnu* and said,
"I'm so honoured that you have
chosen me for this. I will do as
you say."
He then set to build the ark.

female of every kind of animal and bird on earth, and took them to the ark. He then boarded the ark himself with the *saptarishis*.

Soon the storm clouds gathered and heavy rains followed. Floods came to the land all over.

The water got so deep that even the mountains were covered. Everything was destroyed. But the people and animals in the ark were safe.

Suddenly, *Manu* felt a pull – something was tugging at the boat.

He towed the ark across the wild
waters to one high peak which had
still managed to be above the water
level.

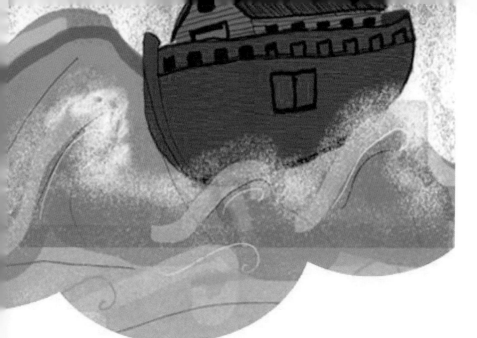

Manu and the ark stay put there for a year.

When the waters receded, *Vishnu* appeared and spoke to *Manu*, "*Manu*, the flood is over. You're now safe ", he said.

the seeds and grow trees. Let the birds and animals build families"

"And you," *Vishnu* smiled at *Manu* "You start a new human race – Let them be called *manav* (man) after *Manu*."

first man on the new earth.
And the father of the human race.

He recorded key principles to lead a
moral life - so the new man does
not become corrupt and wicked as
before - in a book called *Manusmriti*.
But that is another story!

Our universe has three worlds (*loks*). Imagine them as planets.

Swarg Lok

Swarg lok is a heavenly world, where all Gods (*Dev*) live. It is a wonderful place of joy and peace.

Prithvi Lok

Prithvi lok is the world that we live in. Where we perform our deeds (*karma*).
Deeds can be good like being kind and helpful, or bad such as lying, stealing or hurting others.

Narak Lok

Narak lok (Hell) is the home of Demons (*Asur*). It is a horrible place of suffering.

When people die, *Yam* (the God of Death) weighs their good and bad deeds and decides whether they shall go to Swarga or Narak. Good deeds send you to Swarga!

BRAHMA
The Creator

VISHNU
The Preserver

SHIV
The Transformer

Brahma is the **creator** of the Universe. He has four heads pointing to the four directions - north, south, east and west. So, he has knowledge of absolutely everything!
He is married to Goddess *Saraswati*.

Vishnu (or *Narayan*) is the **preserver** of the universe. Whenever world is threatened with evil, *Vishnu* comes in an *avatar* to restore order, and preserve the universe. He has 10 *avatars* -including *Krishna* and *Ram*.
He is married to Goddess *Lakshmi*.

the universe. He is quite short-tempered (*Rudra*) but is also the most innocent (*Bholenath*). He is also a fabulous dancer (*Nataraj*).

He is married to *Durga* (*Parvati*). *Ganesh, Kartik, Laxmi* and *Saraswati* are his children.

Namo Namo Series

The Namo Namo Series, is aimed at introducing children to Hindu Mythology and rich Indian culture.

The titles in this series are meant to bring awareness of the popular Hindu characters and also, festivals to children by means of the rich stories that have been passed down through generations.

Other Titles in the Namo Namo Series....

Printed in Great Britain
by Amazon

21951610R00023